...TORIAN
APPRENTICE

Editor Louisa Sladen
Editor-in-Chief John C. Miles
Designer Jason Billin/Billin Design Solutions
Art Director Jonathan Hair

© 2000 Franklin Watts

First published in 2000
by Franklin Watts
96 Leonard Street
London
EC2A 4XD

Franklin Watts Australia
14 Mars Road
Lane Cove
NSW 2066

ISBN   0 7496 3663 7 (hbk)
0 7496 3944 X (pbk)

Dewey classification: 941.081

A CIP catalogue record for this book is available
from the British Library.

Printed in Great Britian

The diary of
A VICTORIAN
APPRENTICE

by Dennis Hamley
Illustrated by Brian Duggan

W
FRANKLIN WATTS
NEW YORK • LONDON • SYDNEY

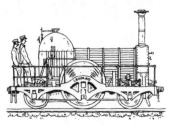

MARCH 14TH, 1846

These are great days in my life, so from now on I shall keep a journal of all the really important things which happen to me. My name is Samuel Cobbett, and I am sixteen years old. I have lived until now in West Fawley, a little village in Berkshire. Soon I'm off to Swindon works, on the Great Western Railway. There I shall start work and perhaps tread in the footsteps of great men famous all over the country. There's Isambard Kingdom Brunel, who built this railway from London to Bristol and gave it rails seven feet apart. That's only right for the great monsters of steam. The narrow gauge other railways are built to is only fit for coal carts. Then there is Daniel Gooch, who came from the north to be top man at Swindon and built the works on marsh and green fields.

My mother cried when I said I wanted to go. My sisters Ellen and Margaret begged me to stay. But I had a great argument with my father. He is the vicar of West Fawley. He's snug in his parsonage with its lawns and gardens and knows nothing of railways. What goes on beyond the village is a horror to him. For his only son to want to be part of it must be a terrible blow.

He said I should go to University and then be a priest like him. I wouldn't do that. I am only sixteen but I know what I want. The railway has changed the world for ever.

I shall go in three days' time. Tomorrow I am to see my father in his study. What he says will decide whether I go with his blessing or whether I walk out of the house and never see my family again. Because whatever happens, *go I will*.

MARCH 15TH, 1846

I will never forget the first day I saw the Great Western Railway. I was only ten. The morning the line was opened, many village people went out to see it, walking ten whole miles to where the rails were laid. One day the rails would reach all the way from London to Bristol, but for now they stretched to Hay Lane, a tiny village, but with its own station and sidings to show that this was the end of the line – for now.

My father forbade me go. He says the railway is an abomination on God's earth and will bring only evil. "What do these railway people want, every fool in London to come to Bristol while every fool from Bristol goes to London?" he said.

But he couldn't stop me. I woke up early and slipped out while everyone slept.

"Your pa won't be too pleased with you," some villagers said. I didn't care. I walked with them all the way until I saw the iron rails shining in the sun and stretching both east and west into the distance. Then, away in the east, we saw a plume of smoke. The rails trembled and hummed with a life of their own. The smoke plume grew larger. Then the shrieking monster was upon us, pounding along the track, huge wheels turning at unbelievable speed. The engine was called *Leopard*. Her tall funnel belched smoke and steam. The fireman shovelled coke into the furnace while the driver watched the way intently. Carriages full of people were strung on behind.

Then I knew what I wanted. I waited until I was sixteen until I disobeyed my father's orders. Will he ever forgive me?

March 16th, 1846

Mr Brunel's and Mr Gooch's new factory at Swindon is the centre of the Great Western Railway and the most modern railway works in the world. On my sixteenth birthday I wrote to Mr Gooch. I was frightened as I posted the letter by the new penny post. What if he tore my letter up? What if he wrote to my father? I might not be let out of the house.

But he did write to my father, well and kindly. It made him think very hard. Today I shall know where these thoughts take him.

The clock in the hall has just chimed the three-quarters. In fifteen minutes I'll knock on his study door. And then I will know.

March 17th, 1846

I can't believe that I go tomorrow. Nor can I believe what happened yesterday in the study. I don't mind saying that I was trembling.

My father stood behind his desk, looking very stern. He said I had grieved him greatly with my love of new-fangledness. But he knew Mr Gooch and Mr Brunel were God-fearing men and he was prepared to let me go, on three conditions. I must find lodgings with respectable people, write home every week, and when I knew what a mistake I'd made I wouldn't let false pride stop me coming home.

I was almost sick with relief. He told me that for the first night I would stay with a clergyman and his wife, the Reverend and Mrs Screde. They would not thank me if I tried to stay there again.

Even though my father let me go, I know I've hurt him. When Mother, Ellen and Margaret saw me off this morning on Jem the carrier's cart, with my little case containing working boots and overalls, he stayed at home. I saw him at his study window but when I waved goodbye he never moved. Now Jem's cart jolts up and down making writing difficult. How I wish Mr Brunel had built his railway through West Fawley so I could be whisked to Swindon in fifteen minutes instead of three hours, which is all old Jem's ancient horse can manage.

MARCH 18TH, 1846 (EARLY MORNING)

Yesterday was hectic. I got off Jem's cart outside the Reverend Screde's rectory. I hope never to endure again such a night of misery. He and his wife said long prayers for me and everyone else who worked for that heathen abomination, the railway works. The house was cold, the dinner awful, the bed lumpy. I hope I find good lodgings soon so I need never go near the Scredes again!

I must leave early to be at the works' entrance in time. From the Scredes' rectory I can see the station and the great factory. The line to Bristol stretches away to the left and there is a train steaming along it. Beyond the station, the line to Gloucester and Cheltenham curves away. Swindon works lies in the angle made by the junction between the two. The great, long workshops, the smoke from boilers and steam hammers – even from here the busy noise and bustle make me shiver with excitement!

View of
SWINDON
1846

MARCH 18TH, 1846 (NIGHT)

Well, the first trial is over and now I'm writing in a strange bedroom by candlelight. I can't help feeling I've done well today. Was I lucky? Yes, I was. But perhaps it's more than that. Perhaps I really am worth it. My new life has well and truly started.

I was told to join the line of men waiting for employment outside the main entrance. I saw old and grizzled men in dirty overalls, younger men in white corduroy trousers and waistcoats and cloth jackets, a few young boys like me in their best suits, wanting to make a good impression. I joined this queue at the end of a tunnel which stretched under an imposing frontage to a mysterious courtyard within.

There were sarcastic shouts from the older men to the young ones. "You'll have no use for all that finery in there!" "There'll soon be more dirt under your fingernails than you've seen before in your whole life."

Foremen came down the tunnel and looked at the men. They left us boys alone. Sometimes, a man got a nod and he walked inside smiling. Sometimes a shake of the head made the man trail gloomily away. I'm a parson's son, so I know what life is like for the poor. There would be little food in the house that day for that man and his family.

The boy nearest to me spoke. "Are you from Swindon?"

"No," I said. "West Fawley."

"And your father's not a labourer on the farm, either. I can tell that by your voice. What are you here for?"

"Because the railway is the future," I said. It sounded pompous, coming out like that.

"Well, it may be and it may not," he replied. "But I'll tell you this, it's the best-paid work round here."

So not everyone feels like me. Perhaps I should keep my ambitions to myself. Still, he laughed, and said we'd all be the same once we were inside. He told me his name is John Haggard. He has an easy smile and an open face. I liked him at once. His father is a shopkeeper, but that, he said, was no job for him.

When I told him my father was a parson and that was no job for me either, he said he might have known it and they'd be treating me special. When I didn't answer, he told me not to worry, he wouldn't hold it against me. But then, as if to prove him right, a man came down the tunnel, dressed in a suit. He called for me by name and John muttered, "Told you, didn't I?"

I followed this man through the tunnel and across a courtyard surrounded by new buildings from which came strange thumping snorts and clangs. Smoke poured out of chimneys. Then we passed through the engine house. Here I saw many huge engines in their stalls. I felt so happy. This was the heart of Swindon works and it looked as if I would be a part of it.

He led me to a little office. Inside, he sat down and motioned me to sit as well. He seemed very young. But then, Mr Gooch was only twenty when Mr Brunel put him in charge of the whole works.

When he asked me if I wanted to be a locomotive engineer, I answered that I did, more than anything. He had my letter in front of him. He said his name was Edward Snell. Mr Gooch gave my letter to Mr Sturrock, the works manager, who passed it on and told him to see me. "You've let yourself in for hard, dangerous work," he said. "Not what we would think fit for a clergyman's son."

"Times are changing, sir," I answered. "I'm not afraid of it."

He said he liked my answer. What he said next made me feel ashamed. My father had written well of me and they would always take a clergyman's word. "You'll do," he said.

So my father did write. I vowed to thank him as soon as I could. Mr Snell said they would take me on as an apprentice. I would start in the building shop with the fitters and turners, but I would be moved around so I got a good idea of everything. It was how he started. He'd been here three years. He'd come from an engineer's workshop in Bath when he was twenty-two and had already been a fitter, erector and engine inspector. Now he was head draughtsman and could end up anywhere on the railway. That was how Swindon was. It looked after its own.

He told me to report tomorrow morning ready to start with the morning shift. Then he asked me if I had any questions.

I couldn't think of any when I should have hundreds. Except one. "Sir," I said. "I've made a friend here already. His name's John Haggard. He's waiting outside. I would like it if we could stay together."

"You will if I like the look of him," said Mr Snell. "Bring him here."

As I walked back I remembered that I hadn't asked about lodgings. I couldn't bear another night with the Scredes.

John was still there. I told him Mr Snell

wanted to see him, took him to the office and waited outside. John was inside longer than I was, but when he came out he was cock-a-hoop. "I reckon I've got you to thank for that," he said. "He's put me in the wheelshop."

I was pleased he was in, but sorry we wouldn't be together. But he answered, "Yes, we will. I reckon one good turn deserves another. Have you got anywhere to stay yet?"

I told him I hadn't and that I'd forgotten to ask Mr Snell about it.

"That's good," said John. "From now on you'll stay with us."

John led me out of the works, across the railway by a bridge and then into a new, strange place which seemed the very opposite of West Fawley with its cottages spread higgledy-piggledy round a village green. Brand-new houses stood in lines along straight streets. One house was like the next and they reminded me of ranks of soldiers on the march. I knew I was seeing the spirit of the new age just as clearly as on the railway or in the works and to me it looked fine.

John led me through Emlyn Square with its wide green in the middle and then turned right into Bristol Street. On the corner was a little shop. It was crowded inside with railway workers' wives buying provisions. John pushed his way through and said to the man behind the counter, "What ho, Pa. I've brought you a new lodger."

So this was John's father. He was a big man, with a red face. There was something about him I liked at once, especially when he gave me a broad smile of welcome.

MARCH 19TH, 1846 (EARLY MORNING)

I couldn't keep my eyes open last night. But I woke at the crack of dawn, lit my candle stub and started writing by its light. John is fast asleep, but I know I won't sleep again.

John was right about his parents. They gave me a grand welcome. We had mutton chops, cabbage and potatoes and a treacle pudding – enough to weigh you down for a week.

John has a twin sister, Jenny. They have the same brown eyes and hair. All evening, though I tried not to, I was stealing glances at Jenny.

Once our eyes met, she blushed and a piece of treacle pudding must have gone the wrong way because she coughed and choked and John had to slap her on the back. I think I'm going to like Jenny. I wonder if she will like me? I'm glad to be here with John Haggard and his family.

That evening, as Jenny and her mother cleared the table and washed up in the scullery, John, his father and I sat round the fire talking. Mr Haggard wasn't upset because his son didn't want to be a shopkeeper. If he was younger, he said, he'd be working on the railway himself. Besides, it wasn't as if he'd got a shop of his own to leave John.

"Why not?" I asked.

"I'm a servant of the Great Western Railway just as much as you will be. The shop belongs to the railway. I only rent it off them. This is a railway town, New Swindon, and every family you see in my shop gets its living through the railway. When you walk up the streets you're on the Great Western Railway as much as if you were walking along the middle of the rails."

We turned in to bed soon after. They rigged up a bed for me in John's room. Before I slept I wondered about the works, Mr Snell, what it would be like to be an engine builder, whether I would ever design locomotives myself – but chiefly, I have to say, about Jenny.

MARCH 19TH, 1846 (EVENING)

This morning we were up early. Mrs Haggard gave us a good breakfast and bread and cheese and tea to take with us. With our overalls and boots on, we marched to Mr Snell's office. He sent John to the wheelshop and then took me to the building shop. He called the foreman over and told him to show me the ropes and then work me hard.

The foreman's name was William Royd. He never said much but he ruled the building shop firmly.

I soon found out who the fitters and turners were. A steam locomotive has many small parts. Take one away and it won't work. Pistons must fit inside cylinders, levers and handwheels in the cab must do what the driver expects them to and steam pipes must not leak. The turner forms every part exactly to size. The fitter secures all these things firmly where they should be and nowhere else.

I expected to be deafened with noise. But there were no steam hammers, blacksmiths' ringing anvils or belching smoke and steam. Instead there was the rush and hum of wheels turning on lathes, tended by men in overalls and blue cloth jackets called slops. Mr Royd said I must get my own slops. Nobody works in the shop without a blue cloth jacket. That's how people know you're in the building shop. It's something to be proud of.

Inside the
ENGINE SHED

These are great days in the building shop. After years of buying from other firms, the first two engines to be built at Swindon are nearly finished. Mr Royd showed me the first. It's a little engine with three small driving wheels on each side, a goods engine in the *Premier* class. But in comparison with what we saw next, it was nothing.

Swindon's first great express engine. And, Mr Royd said, it would be the first of many. The *Great Western* herself.

The *Great Western* is a wonderful sight. She has massive single driving wheels. The supporting wheels at each end are almost as big as the goods engine's driving wheels. At the front is a tall funnel, at the rear a haycock firebox like a small mountain. I can see it making short work of the seventy miles to London. Just to be near it makes me realise how lucky I am to be here, at my age and at this time!

But the sooner I'm working, the more use I'll be. Mr Royd put me under the care of Josiah Wilks, an engine-builder from Newcastle. It took a while to understand a word Josiah Wilks said. He showed me the Whitworth lathes and measuring gauges and the largest slotting machine ever made. By the shift's end, I wondered whether I'll ever make head or tail of them, let alone use them with Josiah Wilks's skill.

So passed my first day at Swindon works.

There was so much to think about, yet once back at the Haggards' shop I was only wondering whether I would ever have a proper conversation with Jenny. The others always seem to be there!

MAY 29TH, 1846

I like living with the Haggards. Their house over the shop is small and the furniture is cheap, not like the heavy stuff at home. Hanging on the walls in frames are samplers Jenny has stitched over the years – *Bless This House* and *God Is Our Strength*. There's no maid or cook: Mrs Haggard and Jenny are cook and maid in turn and we help when we can – as long as we don't interfere with the pots on the kitchen range! But there's happiness and good fellowship here. At night, Mrs Haggard might play the piano and we stand round it singing ballads and hymns.

Or Jenny will read to us, perhaps from one of the new works by Mr Dickens, like *The Pickwick Papers* or *The Old Curiosity Shop*. Sometimes, as she reads, I see her looking at me out of the corner of her eye and I wonder if she thinks that her reading sounds poor to a parson's son who went to grammar school. Well, it doesn't. Her voice is beautiful. To me, it is how an angel would speak. I wish I could tell her so.

JUNE 5TH, 1846

I learn fast with Josiah Wilks. He is impatient sometimes, but it's hard using a lathe or a drill when you're just starting. The men are suspicious of new apprentices. The works are new and there are still few of us. I get jokes and remarks like, "Never thought our jobs could be done by boys." They've come here from all over England, Wales and Scotland. They've made steam engines for railways, pumping stations and ships, so what must they think about a village parson's son still wet behind the ears doing their job?

I said this to Josiah, but he told me to take no notice. They may build engines but their fathers worked on the land and their fathers before them. Back home they'd touch their forelocks to the parson. I disagreed. Any one of them is worth ten of me, parson's son or not. That's part of how the world is changing.

More and more, Josiah is letting me do jobs

unsupervised. Today I completed the whole boring-out of a cylinder for a *Premier* goods engine. This has to be exactly right, because a piston will move up and down inside it for many thousands of miles. When it was done, he looked at it carefully and then said, "It'll do." Nobody ever said such a wonderful thing to me in my whole life.

When John and I got home, Mr Haggard said, "Everybody's talking about the dance this weekend at the Mechanics' Institute. I suppose you three young ones will be going?"

I looked at Jenny and thought, Won't I just!

JUNE 9TH, 1846 (MORNING)

Last night I went to sleep thinking about the Mechanics' Institute dance. When I woke up, my first thought was – it's the great dance tonight. But all night I'd had other, unwelcome, thoughts. What if Jenny already has a beau? What if she's spoken for but she's too shy to tell me? Wouldn't John have said something? I've never breathed a word about what I think of Jenny, but he must have some idea. Yet if that's true then Jenny must know as well. If so, surely she wouldn't let me suffer in silence if she already has a sweetheart?

Well, I'll probably know all after the Mechanics' Institute dance.

June 9th, 1846 (Evening)

I'm writing a few words before we all go to the dance. I'm in the bedroom to put my good suit on.

Josiah was not pleased with me today. I couldn't concentrate on my work. "Wake up, boy, or I'll ask Mr Royd to have you put with the blacksmiths instead," he shouted. That brought me to my senses. Tales of what goes on in the smiths' shop would keep you awake at night. So I pulled myself together. Now it's nearly time to go and I can hear my heart pounding. How will I be feeling when we get home again?

Here's John coming. So under the pillow my diary goes.

June 10th, 1846 (Morning)

I'm writing by the light of my candle stub. John snores away as if the crack of doom wouldn't wake him. I haven't slept much. Last night's events go round and round in my head.

We went, all three of us, to the dance at eight o'clock. It was like going back to work. A room over the building shop had been cleared for the dance. It seemed strange to find such a place decorated with a band at one end and refreshments at the other. I heard muttering about beer and spirits not being sold, but the company would never let strong drink be served on railway premises and if they did, Mr Braid, tonight's Master of Ceremonies and Secretary to the Institute, would soon put a stop to it.

Jenny wore a flowery dress she had made herself. I thought she looked wonderful. She never looked at any man, though I noticed that a lot of men looked at her, me included.

The band struck up. It made a good noise, although just a piano, violin, trumpet and trombone. I saw a few men still looking at Jenny – especially Albert Jones from the smiths' shop. I wanted to pluck up courage to ask Jenny for the first dance but my feet were rooted to the spot and my tongue stuck to the roof of my mouth.

Then – horror! – Albert Jones crossed the floor towards her. What could I do?

Suddenly, someone was speaking: "Get in there quick before that great lump Jones does." It was John. So he has noticed.

I found courage and was there before Albert. He looked furious.

"May I have this dance?" I asked Jenny. "Yes, of course you may," she answered, just as if she expected it. We joined the quadrille and after that we danced together all night.

The time flew past. When we stopped dancing we sat side by side and laughed and joked. I bought a little bowl of sweets and we ate them together. It was as if we had known each other all our lives. I only had one bad moment. Jenny left in the interval with some other girls and Albert walked up to me. He's huge with brawny arms and looks as strong as an ox.

"Look here," he said. He really did sound angry. "Nobody dances with the same girl all night unless they're engaged. Well, nobody's told me anything about that. Are you, you vicar's brat who's only been here five minutes?"

"No," I stammered. "Of course we aren't. I'm only sixteen." I felt a little frightened, I must admit. He was glowering at me as if for two pins he would hit me.

"Then it's about time you gave someone else a chance," he said.

But I wasn't going to, because I didn't like the look of him and I knew Jenny wouldn't. So I answered, "Isn't it up to Jenny who she dances with?"

"We'll see about that," he replied, but just then Jenny came back. I think she must have known at once what had happened, because she just said, very sweetly, "Good evening, Albert," then she turned to me and said, "Aren't you going to ask me for the next dance, Samuel?"

Albert stalked off. He was angry. I reckon I've not heard the last of that.

Perhaps I should have said I was no brat and offered to fight him. But John was happy. He had paired off with Betty Phelps, whose father was an engine repairman. When it was time to go we all went home together. John walked Betty to her parents' house in Exeter Street, leaving Jenny and me outside the shop talking quietly on the doorstep.

She said she'd had a lovely evening, all thanks to me. I said no, not at all, the pleasure was all mine. Then she held my hand and I wondered about kissing her on the cheek. But I didn't dare!

John was soon back. Mr Haggard let us in, Jenny went to her room, John and I went to ours, I tumbled into bed and my mind hasn't stopped racing since.

June 12th, 1846

I have not seen much of Mr Snell since I joined. He has been on a business trip for the company, but now he is back and will soon be promoted again. This morning he came into the building shop and spoke to William Royd, who called me over, to Josiah's annoyance. I was to be shown round the rest of the works, to get an idea of what went on everywhere.

Mr Snell said I would see the different parts of the works over the next few days. I remembered what John had said, that they'd be treating me special. That made me feel a bit bad, because I didn't want it – and yet in a sort of way I knew I did.

First he took me to the boilershop. I am thankful I don't work there. The noise is terrible, with hammers banging in rivets and stays. I could never stand it. Mr Snell told me to think of the poor boilersmiths hammering rivets inside the boilers. They end up deaf with all that row echoing in such a tiny space. There are hundreds of rivets and each must be perfect. Otherwise, the boilers would explode and drivers be killed.

This has happened, though thankfully not yet at Great Western. What would happen to the families that were left? As a clergyman's son I have visited poor families in his parish with him and I know what poverty is like when the breadwinner is gone.

Then I saw the smiths' shop and the foundry

and it was no wonder that I couldn't hear myself speak when the shift was over. Just as well. I couldn't make out what Albert Jones shouted at me in the smiths' shop.

So I went home – that's how I think of the Haggards' shop now – and told them of my day and John said I didn't know the half of it yet. But I think I do, or at least, some of it.

June 13th, 1846

Today, Edward Snell told me about his business trip. He had been round factories and foundries in the north looking for new ideas. He had found some, but came home sure that Great Western ways were the best. He said how fast and smooth broad-gauge expresses are compared with the bumpy, slow old narrow-gauge trains. He told of the chaos at Oxford and Gloucester stations where the gauges meet and everything has to be unloaded from one train to another. But he also said that though the way we do things is better, the way others do them is cheaper. One day Great Western must convert to the narrow gauge like the rest.

I couldn't understand why. Surely seven feet between the rails must be better than less than five feet? "I believe what's best must win through in this world," I said. "That's what a boy with a clergyman for a father is taught to think," he answered gloomily. "Don't you believe it."

JUNE 14TH, 1846

Today I was in the wheelshop. John's foreman let
him show me round. The separate parts for each
wheel, spokes, rim and centres, are forged
separately in wrought iron and then welded
together. I asked why they aren't forged in one
piece like the parts we make in the building shop.
He said wrought iron wouldn't stand the strain.
If steel could be made in big enough quantities
they could be done like that because steel
wouldn't break.

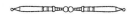

JUNE 17TH, 1846

Well, my tour of the works is over and I've seen
everything that goes to make a railway locomotive.
It ended in the erecting shop. Here a travelling
crane is suspended from the roof and runs right
down the middle of the shop. It carries finished
boilers and lowers each one gently on to its frame.
The engine takes shape and will come alive as soon
as the furnace is lit and steam enters the cylinders.
Mr Snell asked me what part of what we saw
interested me most and I answered, "Everything."
What I wish for most, as much as marrying Jenny
one day, is to be able to say as an engine leaves the
works, "I made that. It's my locomotive."

"Mr Stephenson and Mr Gooch felt like that
when they were young," said Mr Snell. "It seems
to me that you don't just want to put engines

together. You want to design them. Is that true?"

I admitted that it was.

"Good," he answered. "One day you may have your chance. Work hard, take whatever extra training is offered and you'll get good promotion here. Remember what I said. 'Swindon looks after its own.'"

JULY 22ND, 1846

I've been working on the Great Western Railway for a few months. The men know and accept me. We have good laughs and the jokes aren't against me now. Josiah trusts me to do a good job. But I keep thinking of what Mr Snell said last month. I enjoy it with the fitters and turners and get on with the men but I chafe for wider horizons and places where decisions are made.

JULY 24TH, 1846

It is Sunday and very sunny. Today, while John helped his father set out shelves in the shop, Jenny and I went for a walk. I felt guilty about leaving them working. John works hard in the wheelshop, but he said he must help his father too. Jenny thought she should help her mother, but Mrs Haggard wouldn't hear of it. For us to go on a walk alone together was their idea, not ours. It was something I would never have dared to think about. We walked for miles, by the canal and across fields, and at last we talked.

Jenny told me all about going to the little church school where she learnt to read, write and do arithmetic and needlework, and I told her what it had been like to go to grammar school and learn Latin and Greek, though much good they were doing me now, unlike her education. There seemed so much to say because our lives have been so different, yet for a long time my tongue seemed stuck and I couldn't utter a word.

It was a lovely afternoon, except for one thing. Coming home, we passed a cricket match going on. The fielder on the boundary was Albert Jones. When he saw us, his face darkened. "I'll take that smile off your face, vicar's brat," he growled. Jenny told me to take no notice. But it isn't easy with a great brute like that watching me.

JULY 25TH, 1846

Sensation on the main line! The *Great Western* has shown she's the fastest, most powerful engine in the world – but she has broken her front axle at Shrivenham. Too much weight on the front carrying wheels. So she is to be altered, to have four carrying wheels on the front end and longer frames. New express engines, like the *Iron Duke* which is nearly ready, will be the same.

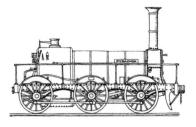

MARCH 18TH, 1847

I see it's the best part of a year since I started to write my diary. Things have passed by in such a whirl that I have hardly had time to think, let alone write. I must do better in future.

We are just home from a lecture at the Mechanics' Institute. Mr Philip Hatch came from London to tell us about "The Genius of Boz", Mr Charles Dickens, who was making the whole nation laugh with Mr Pickwick and cry with Oliver Twist and Little Nell. Jenny said we must go because of all her reading of Dickens to us. But we couldn't think about that for long. There are terrible rumours around about what might happen to us all.

MARCH 19TH, 1847

Monday today, so back to work. Everyone is worried. It seems the railway boom is ending. For the first time railway companies are losing money. There is no need for so many engines. Just as we are ready to build hundreds, we only want a few. Not as many people are travelling by train as we thought would. The Bristol and Exeter Railway, a separate company from the Great Western Railway, does not want us to build and repair their engines any more. Less work means fewer workers. What will happen to us?

MARCH 20TH, 1847

Albert Jones follows me around. Luckily, there are always friends with me when he is there. But I know he's watching me even when I don't see him. Why doesn't he challenge me to a fight over Jenny? No, he has something else up his sleeve for me.

MARCH 24TH, 1847

Another dance tonight. Everybody can see now that Jenny and I are inseparable. Albert looks at me with fury in his eyes. How can he be so jealous yet do nothing about it? His mates tease him and egg him on to action. I didn't like what I saw and took Jenny home early lest he waylaid us.

MARCH 29TH, 1847

I'm home, bruised and shaken. Things were strange in the shop this morning. People were quiet. I felt uncomfortable all day. Even Josiah cleared his throat before he told me what to do as if he didn't want to talk to me. When we stopped for our break, Arthur Worsley, a turner from Manchester, spoke to me. "Don't worry," he said. "The lads in here are on your side." I didn't know what he meant then.

But going home I did. We walked out together. I lingered outside the wheelshop, waiting for John. Then we crossed the works, passed the foundry and the coke heap outside.

"There's something wrong," said John. "The place is deserted. It's much too quiet."

Suddenly there was a shout of "There he is!" Men poured out from behind the coke heap. Smiths, every one. John shouted, "Run!" But it was too late. They were close upon me.

But I wasn't alone. More men poured out of the wheelshop. My own mates from the building shop charged from the other way. They managed to surrounded John and me so the smiths couldn't get to us. I heard Josiah shout, "Don't dare touch him. You'll have to take us on too!" Albert shouted, "Why are you hiding a vicar's brat who steals our women?" Josiah answered,

"Sam Cobbett's our friend. If a girl likes him that's her choice, not yours. Now, go home, the lot of you."

The smiths are brawny and strong. Our people are wiry and small by comparison. But there are twice as many of us. I know just how strong anyone working in our shop has to be. The smiths knew they were outnumbered. They turned away, though not before Albert shouted, "I'll not forget this, Sam Cobbett!" I didn't think he would. He means me harm.

As we walked home, John said that it was as well there wasn't a fight. If the managers had found out we'd all have been sacked. I knew he was right, but I reckoned I hadn't heard the last of Albert Jones. How can I stop him picking a fight with me?

NOVEMBER 26TH, 1847

Another long gap since I wrote anything. All the time we have been waiting to see whether the slump that seems to have hit the railways will reach the Great Western. It doesn't seem eight months that I wondered what would happen to us. Things have gone on as usual, but anyone can see there is worry and doubt in people's eyes. Now we know. The first men are being laid off. Twenty smiths and foundrymen and ten engine erectors went yesterday. None of us is safe. Building work on the new shops has stopped. Will they ever start again?

November 30th, 1847

Today, the worst happened for the Haggards. Men are being laid off in the wheelshops. John is one of them. "Last in, first out," he said bitterly when he came home. "It looks like I shall have to be a shopkeeper after all."

Mr Haggard said he should be pleased. At least he's got a job to go to. What chance of work did the other poor devils have?

All night I lay awake, sad for John and worried lest they would cut the fitters and turners. Would it be last in, first out for me as well?

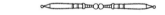

December 3rd, 1847

Twelve in our shop were laid off today. Josiah was safe. He's too experienced to lose. I escaped as well. There were some angry looks that I, a mere apprentice, was kept on, while experienced men with families were told to go. I nearly volunteered to take the place of one of them. Josiah stopped me and told me not to be a fool. When I got back to the Haggards', John was bitter. "I always knew they'd be treating you a bit special," he said. I do not want to believe it but I fear he's right.

December 5th, 1847

I was not much cheered to hear that Albert Jones is laid off. I'm sorry for him. I'm also afraid about what he might do now I am kept on.

December 18th, 1847

Christmas will be sad for the Haggards. Worse still, I shudder to think what it will be like for the families of men in Swindon with no jobs. Progress is a wonderful thing, but it causes heartache on the way.

December 19th, 1847

I think I know now why I was not laid off. Mr Snell called me to his office today. Mr Sturrock, the works' manager, was there as well. He spoke first. "Cobbett," he said. "Tell me what you told Mr Snell the day your tour of the works finished." I thought back to the day and said, "I made that. It's my locomotive."

"You mean you want to be a locomotive superintendent?" Mr Sturrock asked me, stroking his beard. I said yes. He told me the only place to get a whole view of the works and also the place where designs were made was the drawing office. Then he said, "Why not leave the building shop and become a draughtsman?"

My first thought was that I would be sorry to leave Josiah after all that he had done for me. But this was a wonderful chance for me.

DECEMBER 20TH, 1847

John wasn't pleased with my news. He muttered about one law for the rich, which upset me to hear. But Mr and Mrs Haggard were happy for me and Jenny whispered, "Don't worry. John will stay your friend if you want him to." Of course I want him to. He's the best friend anyone could have. Then she said, "Please don't leave us. I want you to stay."

This made me feel so happy. I couldn't leave now, could I?

DECEMBER 21ST, 1847

Today was my last day with the fitters and turners. I told Josiah I was sorry to leave. "Don't be daft, lad," he said. "You'll go far here, and the best of luck to you. I'm always your friend, you can count on that. You did a big thing coming here from the vicarage and you'll go a long way. And we're all behind you." We shook hands and I knew he meant it. So did the rest as they gave me a good send-off with a chorus of "For he's a jolly good fellow". I felt a lump in my throat.

DECEMBER 22ND, 1847

Today I started in the drawing office. Compared with the building shop, it is so quiet. It will take time to get used to. But I may have done some good.

I expected to see drawings of new locomotives. There were a few *Iron Duke* and *Premier* class goods engine drawings, but mostly I saw drawings of bridge girders, point levers and trucks. Mr Snell told me that to keep the works going, they were looking for outside work to do for other railways. I asked him if that will mean new workers. He said there might be a few taken back on. So for the second time I spoke on behalf of John. "If trucks are to be made," I said, "you will need men in the wheelshop. If the works are to go forward you will need apprentices. Please, I beg you, take John Haggard back."

Mr Snell said I was right about the works and he admired the way that I spoke up for my friend. He would speak to Mr Sturrock that day. But I don't suppose anything will come of it. At least I tried.

DECEMBER 24TH, 1847

I couldn't believe the news when I came home tonight. Mr Snell and Mr Sturrock took me seriously. They've taken John back on. He and several others start again in the wheelshop on the first day of the new year.

So Christmas will be good after all.

When 1848 comes it will be a better time for many, with much to look forward to. Jenny and John came into Swindon this evening with me to see me off home for Christmas. Before I got on Jem's cart we exchanged little presents and then John said, "Go on, Sam, kiss her. I don't mind." So I did and Jenny kissed me back and I knew that my Christmas would be perfect, even without Jenny.

MARCH 10TH, 1848

This year is not proving so wonderful after all. Last year, nearly two thousand men worked here. Now there are barely six hundred. Wages have been cut. We are all on short time of forty-five hours a week. The works echo with emptiness. New Swindon is half-deserted. Mr Haggard looks gloomily at his empty shelves and few customers come in to the shop. Many have left as men go away to seek new work. But will they find any? The whole country, we hear, is gripped by this new poverty.

But I'll stay on. I don't believe Swindon is finished or that railways, the greatest invention in the history of the world so far, are doomed, as so many seem to think. People will always need to travel.

March 21st, 1848

It's not all gloom in the drawing office. At least we have some new engines to build. The *Premier* goods engines are always being improved. So are the *Iron Duke* express engines. Everyone knows the *Great Western* will prosper again. There's a feeling that with locomotives like these to build things can't be bad for ever.

April 4th, 1848

Disease is spreading. Typhus and cholera follow hunger and want and now they have come to the town. Thank heavens the Great Western Railway was farsighted enough to run a medical service for its workers and their families. Mr Gooch thought of it and pushed it through. Some pay a penny ha'penny a week, others pay fourpence. It all depends how much they earn. But everyone who pays sees a doctor and has medicines for free. If we did not have this medical fund, I shudder to think what would happen. Terrible stories come from London about people dying from cholera by the hundred.

April 15th, 1848

The epidemic may be dying down. Things are improving in the works. A few men have been taken on again. I was glad to hear that Albert

Jones was among them – he has been taken on in the rolling mills – and also that he has been seen with another girl. For many months I have gone in fear of him.

AUGUST 19TH, 1848

Tomorrow is Sunday and I have a day off. I'm taking a few minutes to write in my diary because I've been slacking off writing in it again. I have been wondering for a long time what my parents and sisters would think of Jenny. Well, soon now I will know. I asked Mr and Mrs Haggard if they would let me take her to West Fawley. They did not mind as long as someone went with us. They meant a chaperone, like my maiden Aunt Charlotte, who always goes with Ellen and Margaret to make sure no harm comes to them.

But there is no Aunt Charlotte here. Then John said he would come with us and everybody was happy. He will keep an eagle eye on his sister. Early tomorrow we will set off. Jem doesn't run his cart on Sundays. We have a five-mile walk to start with, then we will meet Mr Walker, one of my father's parishioners, with his pony and trap to take us the rest of the way. Father asked him to pick us up. He can't do so as he takes services in church all day. Perhaps it will be a relief for Jenny not to see him first thing.

AUGUST 20TH, 1848

Well, now I'm back at the Haggards and feeling quite relieved. Everybody liked John. My mother seemed to think the world of Jenny and Ellen and Margaret loved her. Jenny was quiet and demure and made a very good impression. I feared that because she was a shopkeeper's daughter they would look down on her, but if they did, they kept it to themselves. Good, because she's the only girl for me!

As we walked and then met Mr Walker with his pony and trap, Jenny was silent. Only when we reached the parsonage did she whisper to me, "Sam, I'm frightened."

I told her there was no need to be – and of course as far as my mother and sisters were concerned, there wasn't. But my father – that's a different matter.

We went to morning service. When I saw him in cassock and surplice, wearing his university hood, I tried to look at him through Jenny's eyes and he seemed forbidding indeed. He came in for lunch and hardly looked at or spoke to her. He said grace, ate silently, then went into his study. "I have this evening's sermon to write," he said.

Only when we were about to leave did he appear again. He shook hands with John affably enough. But he looked severely at Jenny, made a slight bow and said, "I am very pleased to have met you, my dear." The look he cast at me seemed to say: I'll have words with you when we next meet, my son.

That is my only worry. Is he going to be difficult? Does he want me to marry some bishop's daughter one day? How I hope not.

OCTOBER 14TH, 1848

More big news to remember in my diary. Suddenly there's great activity in the drawing office. Mr Brunel has had to admit that his great idea for an Atmospheric Railway powered not by steam but by compressed air to run on the South Devon Railway will not work. The line beween Exeter and Plymouth was built with steep gradients because this useless idea was supposed to make light of them. I'm surprised. Mr Brunel is usually right about everything. But we knew better at Swindon – nothing can beat steam power. Now we have to design new engines which will manage the hills. Our hands will be full for some time and there will be good work in the workshops as well. John's job is safe for a while. So is Albert's. So is mine. What a relief!

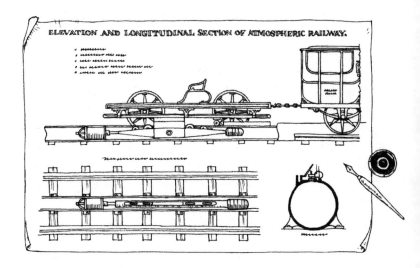

ELEVATION AND LONGITUDINAL SECTION OF ATMOSPHERIC RAILWAY.

NOVEMBER 20TH, 1848

Mr Snell has put me on to helping with the design of some new powerful tank engines for the South Devon Railway. I could learn a lot from this. And it's wonderful that he is trusting me to do it.

December 15th, 1848

Christmas is nearly here again. It's hard to believe. Lots of games, goose and pudding – and perhaps the chance to kiss Jenny under the mistletoe!

December 20th, 1848

Today something happened which I think I shall have bad dreams about for many years to come. I know there have been bad accidents in the works and men have been killed or injured, but till now I never saw one. This morning I paid a visit to the rolling mills with Mr Snell to see the progress of the iron for the frames for the new tank engines. I had forgotten the terrible heat of this place. It hit me as soon as I entered like a blow between the eyes and I nearly fainted. When I recovered I watched white-hot iron conveyed from the furnaces to the steam hammers. How it is done appalled me. Men stagger along with barrows full of the stuff. I saw Albert Jones in this procession. One little sway or loss of balance and they could be done for most horribly by the molten metal. Even as I watched, Albert staggered and lost his grip on the barrow. I could not bear to think what might happen. I dashed forward, dragged him away, saw as if in a dream the barrow tip away from us and this deadly molten stuff spread across the floor. I found strength I never knew I had to pull him to safety and save myself from the metal as well. Quickly others managed to contain the dreadful flood. Albert looked up to see who had saved him from certain death. He smiled at me and said, "So you're good for something, vicar's brat. I owe you thanks and I won't forget." Then he fainted away.

December 24th, 1848

Home again. I need my holiday. The adventure in the rolling mills has taken a lot out of me. But not before Albert Jones and I had a glass of ale together in The Queen's Tap, New Swindon's only public house. "I owe you my life, Sam. As far as Jenny's concerned, you can forget me," he said. "Are we friends?" I asked. "I reckon so," he answered. We shook hands on it and a great weight is lifted from my mind. But there's another taking its place.

This Christmas Day, I know Father will speak to me about Jenny.

DECEMBER 25TH, 1848 (NIGHT)

I was right: Father did speak. He took me into his study and remembered that day two years ago when he grudgingly let me go to Swindon.

"So you wish to marry this Haggard girl?" he said.

"Yes, Father," I answered.

"I believe every man needs a good wife, to settle down with for the whole of his life," he said. "But you are very young," he added.

"Many men marry at my age," I replied.

"That may be so, but they are members of the lower orders," he said. "If you had gone to University as I wished, you would not be able to marry now. If you tried, you would be sent down. Even apprentices, I believe, cannot marry until their seven years are up. Besides, you should wait until you can make a more prudent match."

I found myself answering heatedly. "Jenny *is* a prudent match," I cried. "She's quiet, kind and capable and I care for her dearly. She will give me comfort and support all my life and I will do the same for her. That's more than I could expect from the daughter of a grasping archdeacon, who would expect me to become a bishop or something like that."

I saw pain cross his face. "I am distressed that

you think so ill of my calling," he said.

I had gone too far. "I'm sorry, Father," I muttered. "I did not mean it."

There was a long silence. I saw my dreams crumble before my eyes. Then, to my surprise, he said, "No, son, you may be right. You have entered a world that I do not understand. I can only rejoice that it seems to make you happy. I know the world is changing and I must accept that you are part of that change. Of course you may marry your Jenny. But I ask that you wait until your apprenticeship is over and you know better what your future is. Then I will gladly give you my blessing, because all you say you see in Jenny I can see for myself." He was silent a moment. Then: "I see your mother in her."

I came out so happy. I enjoyed the rest of my Christmas Day to the full. But now I am writing in bed, other thoughts come to mind. My apprenticeship lasts seven years. We must wait until 1853. Will that content Jenny? Will she wait that long for me?

DECEMBER 27TH, 1848

I told Jenny today. She was very quiet for a moment. Then she said, "That's quite all right, Sam. I'll wait. I promise I will." But somehow there's a doubt at the back of my mind and it won't go away. I wish we could marry sooner, because there'll never be anyone else for me.

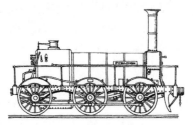

FEBRUARY 15TH, 1849

The new year is well under way and when I look round the works it strikes me how lucky I am. There are hardly seven hundred workers here whereas when I came there were two thousand. Most still here are experienced men. But Swindon will remain. New extensions are being built, even though work is slack.

FEBRUARY 16TH, 1849

Today I realised just how slack things are. Mr Snell has been asked to make watercolour paintings of the works because there's nothing else for the drawing office to do. I am helping him.

FEBRUARY 17TH, 1849

These paintings are to be great panoramas of the works, such as I have been told you can see in the Camera Obscura in Bristol. As Mr Snell made his first sketches today, he said, "I wish I was a high-flying bird, so I could see this scene for myself."

"Perhaps you could go up in a balloon, such as Napoleon's armies used for observation," I replied.

He laughed. "I should be sick with fear," he said. "I'll stay on the ground, as God intended."

MARCH 12TH, 1849

The paintings will be wonderful. What a superb craftsman Mr Snell is.

MARCH 20TH, 1849

The paintings are finished. They are a fine record of these magnificent works in 1849. And I helped in the doing of them.

MAY 20TH, 1849

When Mr Snell finished those paintings, I never guessed they would be the last work he did for the Great Western Railway.

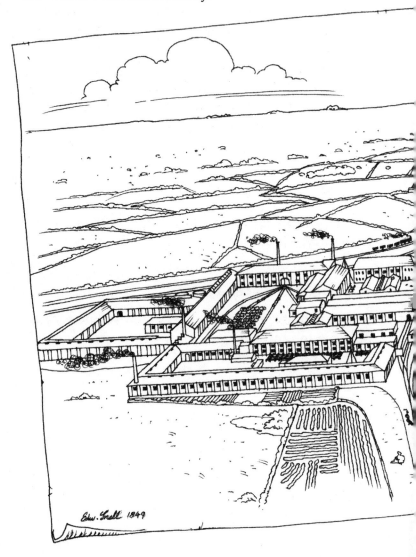

Edw. Snell 1849

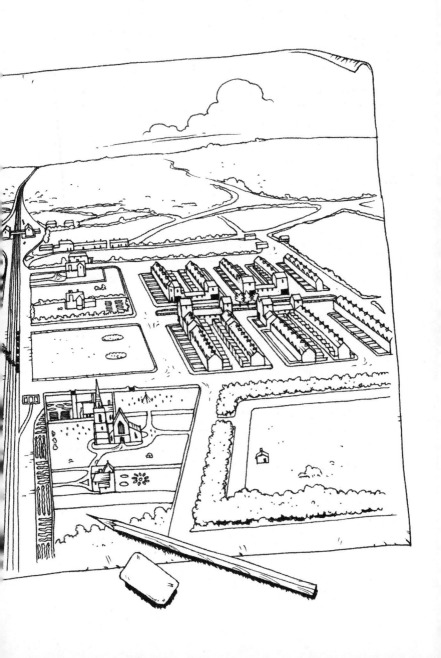

He is leaving and sailing off to Australia. I asked him why. His salary is being reduced from two pounds and fifteen shillings a week to two pounds only. "I can't stomach such a drop and I don't deserve it," he said. "If this is a sign of the times in England, then I shall go to a new country and start again. They need railways in Australia just as much as we do."

I shall be very sorry to see Mr Snell go. He has watched over my career here since I came. Now he's going, I feel really on my own.

AUGUST 15TH, 1849

Things have been quiet for some time, but we had a great day today. The Mechanics' Institute organised a big outing by train to Oxford. Five hundred of us went – workers, wives and lady friends. John came, with Betty Phelps who he has been seeing ever since that first Mechanics dance. I went with Jenny. It was wonderful to be a passenger in a carriage hauled by an engine, both of which I had a hand in designing and building. We had a lovely time in boats on the river and looking round the old colleges. It crossed my mind, though I never told anybody, that if my father had had his way I would have been a student here and not a visitor. I didn't regret it. There's already talk of this being an annual event; perhaps a whole works holiday. We might even have free passes on the railway.

OCTOBER 20TH, 1849

Over the last couple of months I have been
learning more about this wonderful railway
I work for. I love going over the engine sheds and
talking to drivers and firemen, especially those
who have worked for the company since it
started. They tell amazing tales. The best is how
the Great Western Railway caught a murderer
four years ago.

Professor Wheatstone has invented an electric
telegraph, which, it seems, can transmit messages
along electric wires and the railway has fitted the
system between between Paddington and Slough. A
certain John Tawell wanted to get rid of a woman
in Slough once and for all, so he travelled there
from London by train with a phial of poison in his
pocket.

When he met her he poured her a glass of beer and slipped the poison in.

It couldn't have been enough, because once she tasted the foul stuff she screamed at the top of her voice. He at once rushed out of the house straight to the station and caught the first train to Paddington. He was sure that when he was back in London nobody could ever find him. But someone saw him leave the house, so a telegraphic message was sent from Slough to Paddington with his description and he was arrested as soon as he got off at the station in London. He was brought to justice by the power of progress. Perhaps one day there will be telegraphic wires all over the country, so no murderers can ever get away again.

DECEMBER 24TH, 1849

Christmas again. A happy time. The end of the
year has shown work coming back and more men
being employed. The Haggards' shop is
prospering. The line to South Wales will soon be
opened. Extra engines will be needed. Truly the
worst must be over for Swindon works.

April 20th, 1850

Over the last months I have got used to Mr Snell
not being here. But now Mr Sturrock the works
manager is going as well. He is off to Doncaster,
to take charge of engine building for the Great
Northern Railway. He will be equal with Mr
Gooch. I wonder if I will ever be. That's a fine
thought.

September 30th, 1850

Everybody is talking about a Great Exhibition to
be held in London next year, to show off the
wonders of British engineering and marvels
from the rest of the world. Well, if they want the
marvels of British engineering, they should have
their Great Exhibition in Swindon.

October 19th, 1850

Much excitement in the drawing office. We are to prepare drawings for a new express engine, the best of the *Iron Duke* class, the finest ever to run on the broad gauge. What will her name be, I wonder?

FEBRUARY 14TH, 1851

For the last months I have been one of those
making drawings for our new engine and
watching her take shape. She is to be called
Charles Russell after the chairman and will be
exhibited in the wonderful Crystal Palace in
Hyde Park, in the Great Exhibition. How I
would love to go with her, to see the wonderful
building the whole world talks about and the
incredible array of riches the peoples of Earth
can bring forth which it will house.

MARCH 15TH, 1851

Mr Brunel has paid a rare visit to Swindon.
His short figure in a black suit with a tall stove-
pipe hat on his head is well known from

engravings in newspapers. Tomorrow he comes to the drawing office. At last, I will see *the great man himself.*

MARCH 16TH, 1851

I cannot believe what has happened. When Mr Brunel entered, everyone was quiet and respectful. He looked at drawings for the new engine. He picked one set up, scanned it carefully and then said, "Who did these?" I recognised *my own drawings.* My heart beat fast. He must have found something wrong. Mr Minard Rea, who had succeeded Mr Sturrock as works' manager, said, "Young Cobbett, sir." "Let me see him," said Mr Brunel. I walked towards him wanting to die on the spot. He would berate me for an incompetent fool and dismiss me at once.

But no. "I am impressed," he said. "These are excellent." I was tongue-tied. I felt as if I was in the presence of God Himself. "You have done well, Cobbett," he continued. "I will reward you. We need bright young men at the Crystal Palace to explain the mysteries of our engine to the world. How would visiting London with the *Charles Russell* appeal to you?"

I could only answer, "Very much, sir." But then I thought of Jenny and John left at home. How wonderful if Jenny could come too. No, that would not be seemly. But what about John? It was now or never, because if I asked Mr Rea later I would get a short and dusty answer. I plucked up courage and said, "Sir, I would very much like to go with a friend and someone my own age." I could see Mr Rea looking daggers at me. But Mr Brunel smiled and said, "Well asked, Cobbett. Who have you in mind?" "My good friend John Haggard from the wheelshop," I answered. "He could explain the engine as well as me." "Of course he could," said Mr Brunel. "That you asked shows me you know what you want and strive to get it. I would have asked for the same thing if I were you and your age again."

So it is settled. John and I are off to London together to see the Great Exhibition. We will stay there for three weeks and then two more young ones will be picked to come and take our places. When I told John, he couldn't speak for amazement and delight.

APRIL 11TH, 1851

The Chairman doesn't want an engine at the Exhibition named after him. He says we should honour Prince Albert, whose idea it all was. So instead, our great engine will be called *Lord of the Isles,* a name which will last for ever.

APRIL 23RD, 1851

There's been no time to write these last weeks. There has been so much to do, preparing for our great adventure. Today we leave for London with *Lord of the Isles.* I said goodbye to Jenny with much regret because we shall be away for a long time. "Don't go near any of those fast women they say live in London," she told me. "You can trust me," I answered. "But don't you go near Albert Jones, either." "As if I would," she said. "Anyway, he's sweet on Mary O'Malley now." I was only joking. I know she wouldn't go near Albert Jones – or anyone else.

APRIL 23RD, 1851 (AFTERNOON)

Now we are on the train. *Lord of the Isles* is making good speed through Didcot. John is on the footplate with the driver and fireman. No other engine in the world can haul a train so fast and no railway in the world can bear the carriages so smoothly and quietly as the Great Western Railway with its broad gauge. I can't believe that one day the wonderful "seven-foot way" will be torn up and the hated narrow gauge will triumph.

At Reading we stop to take on water. John and I change places and I will be with the driver and fireman for the last thirty-six miles.

APRIL 23RD, 1851 (NIGHT)

We have been placed in a boarding house in Eastbourne Terrace, overlooking the goods shed. I have had a momentous day. At Reading, John stepped down from the footplate of *Lord of the Isles* and I took his place. His face was smutty and he said, "Watch yourself up there, Sam." The train left. A warm sun shone down and the furnace pushed heat out so I was sweating at once. I wondered what bad weather would be like at sixty miles an hour with no shelter for the enginemen. I will never forget that hour on the footplate. The noise was tremendous yet the movement was smooth. I watched driver and fireman until the driver said, "Here, you have a go," and the fireman gave me a spare shovel. I had watched his easy swings which took coke to furnace so easily without spilling a lump. It looked easy, so I tried. The weight nearly broke my shoulder, the coke missed and spilled over the floor. "No, like this," the fireman laughed, and next time guided my arms so only a few pieces spilt. I tried again and was better. By Sonning Cutting I could do it and only spill a few lumps each time. But how he could keep that furnace supplied all the way from London to Bristol I have no idea. Truly enginemen are fine people.

Our train was directed not into the station but the goods yard. Here, a crane hoisted *Lord of the Isles* off the rails and on to a huge cart pulled by eight shire horses, which lumbered off towards Hyde Park. Seeing them go so slowly made me realise again just what a wonderful invention railways are.

April 26th, 1851

Today I saw the Crystal Palace. I just can't describe what I felt: such a fairy structure of glass and white columns, airy and light like thistledown yet so strong and firmly built. The Exhibition does not open until the first of May, so we can see the exhibits for ourselves without the press of crowds. Pavilions are here from all over the world. We've seen the great Koh-i-Noor diamond, a floating church with a spire built for seamen in Philadelphia, a knife with eighty blades, an alarm bed which you can set so it pushes you out of it at the time you have to get up. We've seen engines and inventions from all over the world. There are some very clever things from abroad.

But so much looks as if it will only last a while and then you would have to buy a new one, while what is made in Britain looks so solid as if it will last for ever.

The sun shines through the glass and in the middle are three large elm trees which could not be cut down. Everything is colour and bustle and there will never be anything like it again in the world.

APRIL 29TH, 1851

A great honour tonight, but now I am home my mind is troubled. Mr Brunel invited us to his home in Duke Street. He showed us his private office, where all his new projects start. Here he designed the Great Western Railway and his two wonderful steamships *Great Western* and *Great Britain.* Then we went into the house itself, and into his Shakespeare room, with paintings of the characters round the walls. The decoration is very rich and sumptuous – a bit too much, I thought.

So did John, because he never said a word all evening.

We met Mrs Brunel, a very lovely but rather distant lady, and their children, little Isambard who has a limp, Henry and Florence. Mr Benjamin Hawes, Mr Brunel's brother-in-law, was there as well, with his wife and daughter Maria.

I am afraid this is what gives me trouble. Maria was so pleasant, so sweet and gracious to me and she is so beautiful that I could not take my eyes off her. I quite forgot Jenny, for the first time since we had been away. I think Maria liked me as well, because I am sure she smiled at me several times. Besides, talking to her seemed so easy.

John noticed. "I saw you," he said angrily

when we were back at the lodging house. "If you do anything to hurt Jenny, you're no friend of mine and you'll leave our house when we get back." I told him not to be silly, but he only replied, "Just be careful."

All night I thought how strange it was. When father told me to wait to marry, there was a doubt in my mind. I thought it was about Jenny. Now I know it was about me.

May 1st, 1851

Today, Queen Victoria opened the Great Exhibition. Now we work hard explaining the wonders of *Lord of the Isles* to all who stop to listen.

May 10th, 1851

We get some time off. John and I seem friends again, so we roam noisy streets full of cabs and horses and savour the wonders of London. We have been to the new Zoo in Regents Park and seen amazing animals, especially the bears climbing the ragged staff after buns. We went to Madame Tussaud's Waxworks where we saw the severed heads (in wax, of course) of French aristocrats guillotined in the Revolution and even the coach in which Napoleon escaped from

Waterloo. We went to Leicester Square to see the Great Globe, a perfect model of the world, and the Italian Giant who is nearly eight feet tall, and then to Newcastle Street to hear the Wonderful Singing Mouse.

But all he seemed to do was squeak a bit, so we both thought that was a swindle. One evening we had a Two Shilling French Dinner at Soyer's Symposium in Gore House in Kensington. But best of all was Mr Beard's studio in Parliament Street. We had daguerreotypes made of ourselves. To see ourselves photographically as we actually are is a marvel. One day there'll be no need of paintings, drawings and engravings in newspapers.

MAY 26TH, 1851

Our time in the Crystal Palace is nearly at an end.
We have talked to hundreds from all over the
country and the world about our wonderful
engine. But today the only one I was looking for
came. Maria Hawes, looking elegant and pretty.
But she was on the arm of a rich-looking young
man and her parents were with her. She showed
no sign of even recognising me and I suddenly
felt foolish for what I thought that evening at
Duke Street. John saw her, but never mentioned
it. So I shall forget the whole thing.

But tonight, I feel sad.

MAY 31ST, 1851

We are back in Swindon and our great adventure
is over. Once I saw Jenny, I realised just how
stupid my thoughts about Maria were and Jenny
will never know them.

December 31st, 1852

I have been very busy for a long time and to my shame have just not found time to write anything at all for the whole of this year. Shame on me! But now I must, because important days are coming close.

I cannot believe that it was a year and a half ago since I was in London. Tonight marks the end of my last full year as an apprentice. In less than three months I will be out of my indentures. I shall be twenty-three years old. Swindon has been busy this last year and I have learnt very much. The Great Western Railway has grown. It has bought several narrow-gauge railways and their engines have been sent for repair, much to everybody's disgust. We might even have to build some for the northern parts of the railway. Still, it is all work!

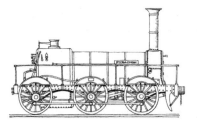

MARCH 16TH, 1853

Today is the day. Now I am fully qualified to seek a position on this railway or any other. What will the years bring forth?

Well, first, as soon as I have a good post, I shall ask Jenny to marry me and now nobody can say a word to stop me. Mr Haggard will give his consent. He and I are great friends. I shall probably stay in Swindon because the Great Western Railway is my first love. But railways have spread all over the world and British engineers have made them, so who knows?

Yes, a great life beckons. The world is progressing and I shall be part of that progress.

FACT FILE

APPRENTICES

The idea of introducing young people to the
mysteries of particular crafts over a long
period of time goes back to ancient days.

For centuries, this "apprenticeship" lasted
seven years. Contracts called "indentures"
were signed by parent and employer and the
apprentice promised several things – not to
give away the secrets of the craft, to be sober
and industrious, not to marry.

When the seven years were up, the
apprentice was "out of his indentures" and
was qualified by experience to practise his
craft: as a blacksmith, a wheelwright, a
bricklayer – or as an engine builder.

CHARACTERS

All the people in this book are fictional
except for some very important ones indeed.
Mr Braid, Master of Ceremonies at the
dance, schoolmaster and Mechanics'
Institute secretary, was a real person. So was
Sam's first friend at the works, **Edward
Snell**. He came to Swindon when he was
twenty-two. He started as a fitter, then was
an erector, engine inspector and
draughtsman. Later, he was general

superintendent of the factory and Sturrock's assistant. He did make watercolour paintings of the works in 1849. The first is now in Swindon Art Gallery, the second in the Great Western Railway Museum in Swindon. However, when his wages were cut in 1849 he emigrated to Australia. While he was at Swindon he kept a diary full of little drawings. His descendants found it years later and it provides much information about the early days of Swindon works.

Archibald Sturrock left in 1850. He became famous for his work on the Great Northern Railway which operated out of King's Cross, and built many fine engines at Doncaster.

Daniel Gooch came to the Great Western in 1837 when he was only twenty. His letter of application is in the Great Western Railway Museum. It is still a model for people applying for jobs today. Brunel needed a good locomotive designer because he knew he was not very good at it. Gooch was ideal. He designed a long line of broad-gauge locomotives which were known for their fine design and construction, power, speed and reliability. He based himself at Paddington, not Swindon, so he could oversee the whole system.

Isambard Kingdom Brunel was an amazing person. He can only be called a visionary genius. His work still survives – the whole of the Paddington-Bristol main line and the bridges and tunnels on it, together with Paddington station and large parts of Bristol Temple Meads. The Saltash bridge over the River Tamar west of Plymouth was his last work and perhaps his most brilliant considering the difficulties he had. His ship the *Great Britain*, on show in Bristol, was the first iron-built transatlantic liner which had screw propulsion rather than paddle wheels. The later *Great Eastern*, which did not sail until after he was dead, was by far the largest ship ever built at the time and, if other people's technology had been up to it, would have been a huge success. All ships since have been built on the principles he worked out for those. He saw that railways should think big and the broad gauge of 7 feet would mean faster, more powerful engines and smoother carriages. The first engineers merely took the rail width of the old horse-drawn tramways, 4 feet 8-and-a-half inches, which some said was the width between the wheels of Roman chariots. But Brunel was too late. The country was already covered with railways built to the cheap but slow narrow gauge. In the end, after years of struggle, the Great Western had to be converted to the hated narrow gauge. The last broad-gauge express left Paddington in May 1892. Many fine engines were broken up. Thankfully, neither Brunel nor Gooch lived to see it.

THE FIRST RAILWAYS

The 1830s were years when steam and railways came together. For centuries it was known that horses could pull greater loads in mines and quarries if the trucks, or chauldrons, ran on smooth rails. For many years, simple steam engines had powered pumps in tin mines. Men like Richard Trevithick and later George Stephenson saw steam could power engines for railways. In 1827, the first railway carrying fare-paying passengers, the Stockton and Darlington, was opened. In 1829, the first main line, the Liverpool and Manchester Railway, was surveyed and built by Stephenson. His engine for it, *Rocket*, was the first modern steam engine. Soon railways were spreading everywhere. The revolution in speed after centuries of walking or going on horseback if you were rich enough had come and with it came the start of the modern age.

Rocket

THE GREAT WESTERN RAILWAY

The merchants of Bristol thought their city was the finest and their port the best in the country. They hated seeing Liverpool get an advantage. In 1832 they decided to have their own railway to London.

In 1833 they hired Brunel to build it for them. Brunel was only in Bristol because he had got very drunk when the Rotherhithe Tunnel, the first tunnel across the Thames – still used by underground trains today – was opened. His father built it and Isambard learnt much from him. But he was so ill after the opening ceremony that he came to Bristol to get better. If he had not drunk so much, he would not have been asked to build the railway!

The route went from Bristol, through Bath, Swindon, Didcot and Reading to Paddington.

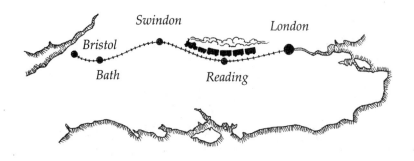

Route of the Great Western Railway

The Paddington station Sam saw was not the one we know now. The line was extended through the goods yard to the present site and Brunel built a station to be better than Euston on the London and North Western Railway.

The new Paddington station was opened in 1854 and is still more or less as Brunel built it, with its wonderful wrought-iron roof. The Box tunnel between Chippenham and Bath was the longest tunnel in the world when it was built.

Train emerging from Box tunnel

In 1838 the first trains ran from London to Taplow. After that it was opened in stages and the whole line was completed in 1841. Over the years the GWR felt it was a cut above the rest. "God's Wonderful Railway", it was called. But detractors, tired of having to go through Bristol to get to Plymouth and Oxford to reach Birmingham, called it the "Great Way Round". Years later the Great Western Railway listened and built faster routes to the west and the Midlands.

In 1948, when the railways were nationalised, the Great Western Railway became the Western Region of British Railways. With privatisation the routes were split up between several companies: nowadays, trains of all colours run where once the engines were green and the coaches chocolate and cream.

SWINDON WORKS

A spot halfway between Bristol and London was needed for engines to be serviced and built. Gooch settled on Swindon. His letter recommending it to Brunel is a fine piece of persuasive argument. Swindon is seventy level miles (112 km) from London and forty-four hilly ones (72 km) from Bristol.

In the first early days, engines were neither powerful nor reliable. Everything stopped at Swindon because an engine change was needed. At Swindon were shedded the large-wheeled fast engines needed for London and the smaller-wheeled powerful ones for Bristol.

Once the site was selected, work went on quickly – first the engine sheds and repair works were built. Then Gooch realised he could not trust builders from outside to keep to his high standards, so he decided Swindon should build its own engines, which it did for 140 years.

The works grew, changed and were developed over the years. Many famous engines were designed and built there – *Stars*, *Saints*, *Castles*, *Halls* and *Kings*. Many still run on preserved railways and sometimes on main lines.

In 1956, Swindon was selected to build the last-ever steam engine for British Rail – *Evening Star*, a 2-10-0 goods engine which has indeed been a star ever since, and is still running.

After the end of steam, diesel locomotives were built at Swindon, but just as the Great Western Railway started off differently from the rest with the broad gauge, so Swindon-built diesels were built on a different principle from all other diesels for British Rail. Instead of diesel-electric transmission they had diesel-hydraulic – in many ways better, but in a minority and more expensive.

By the 1980's it was clear Swindon works would have to go, as railway engineering centred on Crewe, Derby and York. In 1986 it closed for the last time and where the forges, building and erecting shops once were are now business parks, shopping malls and houses. It was the car that finished off the railway as people's main transport and, ironically, Swindon is best known now as a car-producing town.

NEW SWINDON

New Swindon wasn't the first "railway town". Already the London and North Western Railway had built new towns for their workers at Crewe and Wolverton. It was all part of the movement of people from the country to the towns which took place in the nineteeth century as agriculture became less important and manufacturing took over as the chief way of making money.

SMITHS, FITTERS, TURNERS, BOILERSMITHS, ERECTORS, WHEELWRIGHTS, DRAUGHTSMEN

The first railway works tried to make themselves self-sufficient. At Crewe they even made their own rails and station nameplates.

At Swindon they smelted their own iron, including every ounce of scrap. This was melted down in furnaces, rolled out in the rolling mills and stamped into rough dies by the smiths with the huge steam hammers.

The turners fashioned the dies into precision parts – or as near precision as the inaccurate Whitworth measuring gauges would allow – on lathes. The fitters fitted all these parts on to the frames of the engine.

Meanwhile, the wheelwrights had been fashioning the wheels and the boilersmiths, in what must have been the unpleasantest, though not the most dangerous, job, had been hammering the thousands of rivets and hundreds of tubes which went into each boiler. The erectors put the whole together, with the boilers lowered on to the frames to make finished engines.

Then it was off to the paintshops, with fourteen or so coats applied by hand, and finally, out on the rails.

Later on, wheels were bought in from outside and subcontractors did some jobs – but not to start with. The Great Western

Railway wanted to oversee every part of its system.

THE MECHANICS' INSTITUTE

This was a self-help group among the workers and most large factories had one. Not only did it organise dances and social events, but it built up its own library and reading room which became popular at a time when there was no education for all. This did not come until 1871. For most people, if they wanted to have an education, they had to do it themselves. Thousands did.

DISEASE AND THE MEDICAL SERVICE

The medical scheme at the works was very important when public health was poor, water supplies and sanitation appalling and diet was inadequate.

In an age when there was no National Health Service, national insurance, unemployment and family benefit or old age pension, the poor had no protection against epidemics. The scheme which started at Swindon was a forerunner of the National Health Service because the money paid per week worked in the same way that national insurance payments do today.

THE ATMOSPHERIC RAILWAY

This idea appealed to Brunel. It had been
tried in a few places, notably in Croydon.
Brunel saw speed, silence and cleanliness in
it: he didn't realise airtight joints can't be
made with leather kept supple with tallow.
Stationary steam engines pushed compressed
air along a pipe in the middle of the rails.
The train was attached to the pipe and the air
pushed it along. A good theory – but it never
worked properly because the joints kept

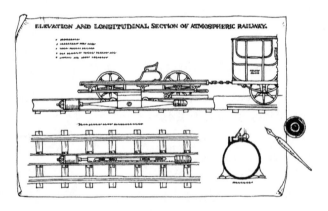

ELEVATION AND LONGITUDINAL SECTION OF ATMOSPHERIC RAILWAY.

leaking. This was a pity, because the South
Devon Railway was deliberately built with
big hills along the route of the track. Brunel
thought the trains would sail across them
and enginemen have cursed it ever since. It
was an idea whose time had not come. If it
was tried today with modern materials, I
wonder what would happen?

WORKS OUTINGS

The first outing by special train to Oxford, which really happened, led to great things. Annual works holidays, excursion trains, free passes for railway employees, even public and Bank holidays – all had their origins in this one day-trip.

THE GREAT EXHIBITION AND THE CRYSTAL PALACE

So much is written about it that there's little to add, except that where Sam and John had their Two Shilling French Dinner has since had the Royal Albert Hall built over it. The Crystal Palace was moved from Hyde Park to Sydenham in south London, where it stayed until it burned down in 1936.

The name exists now as an area and a football club – though Cup Finals were played at the Crystal Palace (not Selhurst Park) before Wembley was built.

SAM, JENNY AND CHAPERONES

Nowadays, their long and decorous courtship sounds incredible. But in Victorian times codes were far stricter. They were just about allowed to go for a walk together near the town – but Jenny would never be allowed to go with Sam to West Fawley on her own. If a maiden aunt was available, she would make a good chaperone. As there wasn't one, John had to do.

West Fawley

No such place. But there are villages called North Fawley and South Fawley, on the downs near Lambourn.

So what about Sam Cobbett?

What did Sam Cobbett do after his apprenticeship ended? He may have stayed at Swindon – but if he did, he never reached the very top. Joseph Armstrong was locomotive superintendent after Daniel Gooch, and William Dean after him. Sam never got a chance.

No. More likely he left to go to another railway to design their engines, as Archibald Sturrock of the Great Northern Railway or James Holden of the Great Eastern Railway did or, the most famous of all, William Stanier, who many years later went to the London, Midland and Scottish Railway and designed famous engines like the *Duchess* Pacifics and Black Fives.

In fact, I know exactly what he did. If you turn to Chapter Six, "Saviours of the

Train", in *The Railway Children* by E. Nesbit, you will see a beautiful picture of the engine which the children saved from the landslide.

I can tell you that it is a 4-4-0 express engine built in 1889 and designed by Samuel Cobbett, then locomotive superintendent of the Great Northern and Southern Railway, because that, after many happy years at Swindon, is where he went in 1875 with his dear wife Jenny.

Jenny and Sam in 1875

OTHER TITLES IN THIS SERIES

THE DIARY OF A YOUNG ROMAN SOLDIER

Young Marcus Gallo is travelling to Britain with his legion to help pacify the wild Celtic tribes. As the Romans march north, Marcus records in his diary how he copes with cold weather, falls in love and narrowly escapes serious injury. Read his diary and find out what life was really like for a young Roman soldier.

THE DIARY OF A YOUNG TUDOR LADY-IN-WAITING

Young Rebecca Swann is joining her aunt as a lady-in-waiting at the court of Queen Elizabeth the First. In her secret journal, Rebecca records how she learns to be a courtier, falls in love and uncovers a plot against the Queen. Read her diary and find out what life was really like for a young Tudor lady-in-waiting.

THE DIARY OF A YOUNG NURSE IN WORLD WAR II

Young Jean Harris has just been hired to train as a nurse in a large London hospital. As Britain goes to war, Jean records in her diary how she copes with bandages and bedpans, falls in love and bravely faces the horrors of the Blitz. Read her diary and find out what life was really like for a young nurse on the Home Front in World War II.